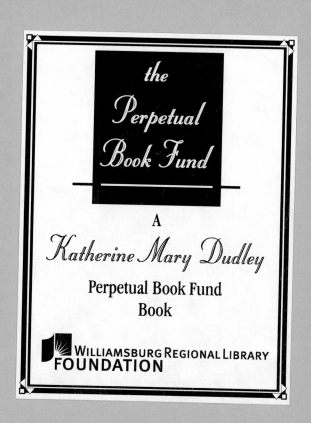

SOMETIMES

YOU GET WHAT YOU WANT

art by Lisa Brown *words by* Meredith Gary

HarperCollins*Publishers*

Sometimes You Get What You Want
Text copyright © 2008 by Meredith Gary
Illustrations copyright © 2008 by Lisa Brown
Manufactured in China.
All rights reserved.
No part of this book may be used or reproduced
in any manner whatsoever without written permission
except in the case of brief quotations embodied in critical
articles and reviews. For information address HarperCollins
Children's Books, a division of HarperCollins Publishers,
1350 Avenue of the Americas, New York, NY 10019.
www.harpercollinschildrens.com

Library of Congress Cataloging-in-Publication Data is available.
ISBN 978-0-06-114015-0 (trade bdg.) — ISBN 978-0-06-114016-7 (lib. bdg.)

Book design by Alison Donalty
1 3 5 7 9 10 8 6 4 2
❖ First Edition

To Brian and Audrey
—M.G.

To Charlotte
—L.B.

Sometimes you get to wear what you want.

Sometimes you don't.

Sometimes you can stay outside.

Sometimes you need to go in.

Sometimes your friends want to do what you're doing.

Sometimes they want to do something else.

Sometimes it's your turn.

Sometimes you have to wait.

Sometimes you can make as much noise as you want.

Sometimes you have to be quiet.

Sometimes you get to eat what you want.

Sometimes you don't.

Sometimes you get to sit next to the person you want.

Sometimes you don't.

Sometimes you get to make a mess.

Sometimes you have to clean up.

Sometimes you can stay awhile.

Sometimes you have to go home.

Sometimes you can do it yourself.

Sometimes you need a little help.

Sometimes you have to go right to sleep . . .

. . . but sometimes you don't.